Michele:

the Nursing Toddler

Michele:
the Nursing Toddler

A story about sharing love

by Jane M. Pinczuk
illustrated by Barbara Murray

La Leche League International
Schaumburg, Illinois

© 1998 La Leche League International
First printing, September 1998
ISBN 0-912500-40-9
Library of Congress Card Number-98-067505
Printed in the USA
All Rights Reserved

La Leche League International
Post Office Box 4079
Schaumburg IL 60168-4079 USA
www.lalecheleague.org

*To my husband, Murray, and the rest of my
family as well as other nurturing families of the world.*

*A special thanks to Barbara for her heartfelt illustrations and
tireless work.*

I have a little story to tell,
about a girl I know very well.

She's so polite and knows NOT to yell;
the name of that special girl is Michele.

Michele is so proud of the things she can do.

I bet if you're a big girl or boy you can do them too.

Like having a friend share a toy with you,
or hiding behind a tree and playing peek-a-boo.

Do you remember when you were very small?
There were NOT many things you could do at all.

You drank milk from your Mom and had hugs from your Dad.

Can you believe that milk was the only food you ever had?

To get from place to place
you had to crawl.

Then learning to walk
meant taking a fall.

Sometimes babies are happy and sometimes they're sad.

But when babies get teeth it makes them REAL glad.

Michele loves her teeth.

She thinks they're neat.

She uses them to smile, talk, and eat, eat, eat!

Yummy foods like bananas,
cookies, carrots, and wheat
make Michele feel good
from her head down to her feet.

Michele enjoys playing with friends
just like you—
as well as painting, dancing, reading,
and going to the zoo.

One thing Michele always knew—
she'll still have lots of love
when her nursing days are through.

As Michele grows older from year to year,
she knows that her loved ones will always be near.

And whether Michele is here or there,

they'll love her and hold her
and show her they care.

About La Leche League International

La Leche League International began in 1956 with a group of seven women who had breastfed their babies and wanted to help other mothers find the joy and satisfaction of giving their babies the best start in life. Since then, their conviction about the importance of breastfeeding has grown into an entire philosophy of parenting which encourages the mother-infant bond established in the breastfeeding relationship. Today La Leche League International is a nonprofit organization devoted to helping mothers around the world breastfeed through mother-to-mother support, education, and information and to promoting a better understanding of breastfeeding as an important element in the healthy development of baby and mother. To find information about a La Leche League Group near you, or to order additional copies of MICHELE: THE NURSING TODDLER contact La Leche League International at 1-800-LALECHE or (847) 519-7730 or write to us at 1400 N. Meacham Road, Schaumburg IL 60173 USA or visit our Website at www.lalecheleague.org/